Clean and Healthy

Nicole Boyd

Rosen
REAL
READERS

Rosen Classroom Books and Materials
New York

To keep yourself **healthy**, you must keep your body neat and clean.

There are many ways to keep your body neat and clean. You can wash with soap and water to get rid of dirt.

You can wash your hands before you eat food and after you use the bathroom. This helps keep your body safe from **germs**.

You can keep the nails on your fingers and toes clean, too. Use a special brush and soap to clean under your nails.

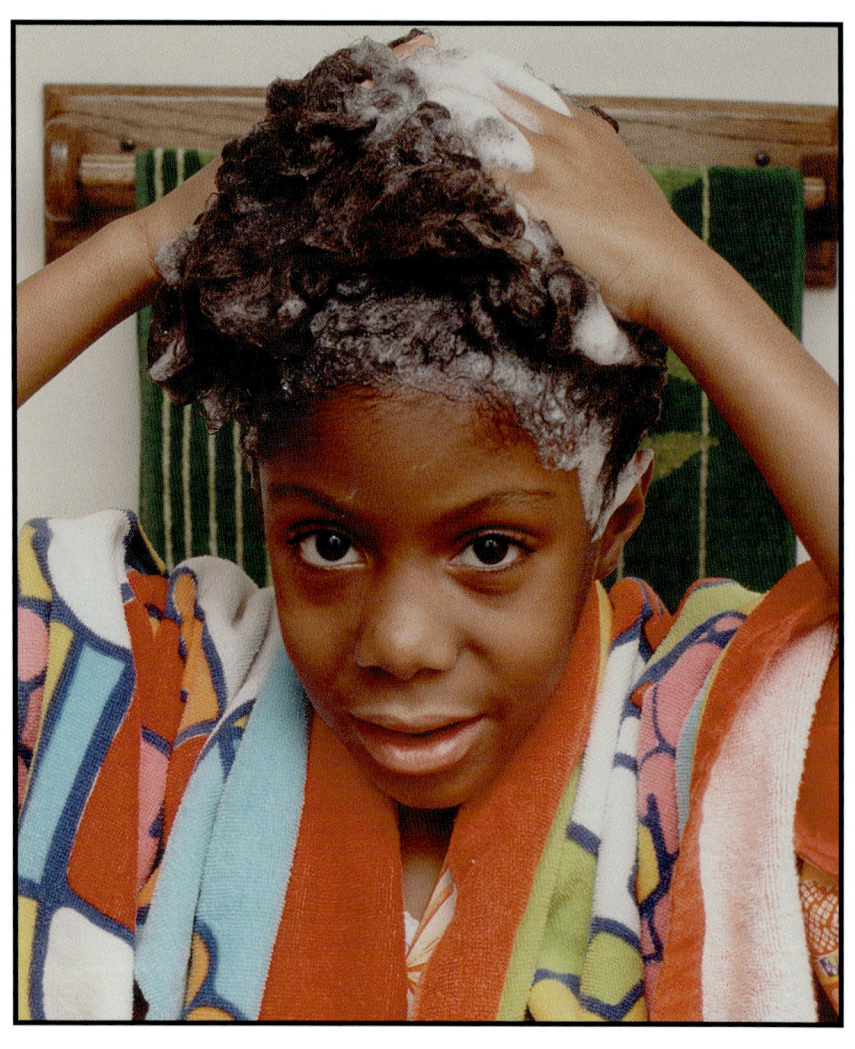

You can wash your hair with
shampoo and water to keep
it clean.

You can comb your hair every
day. This keeps your hair neat
and shiny.

You can brush your teeth and
gums to keep them healthy. You
should do this every morning, after
eating, and before you go to bed.

You can **floss** between your teeth every day. Flossing helps you clean between your teeth.

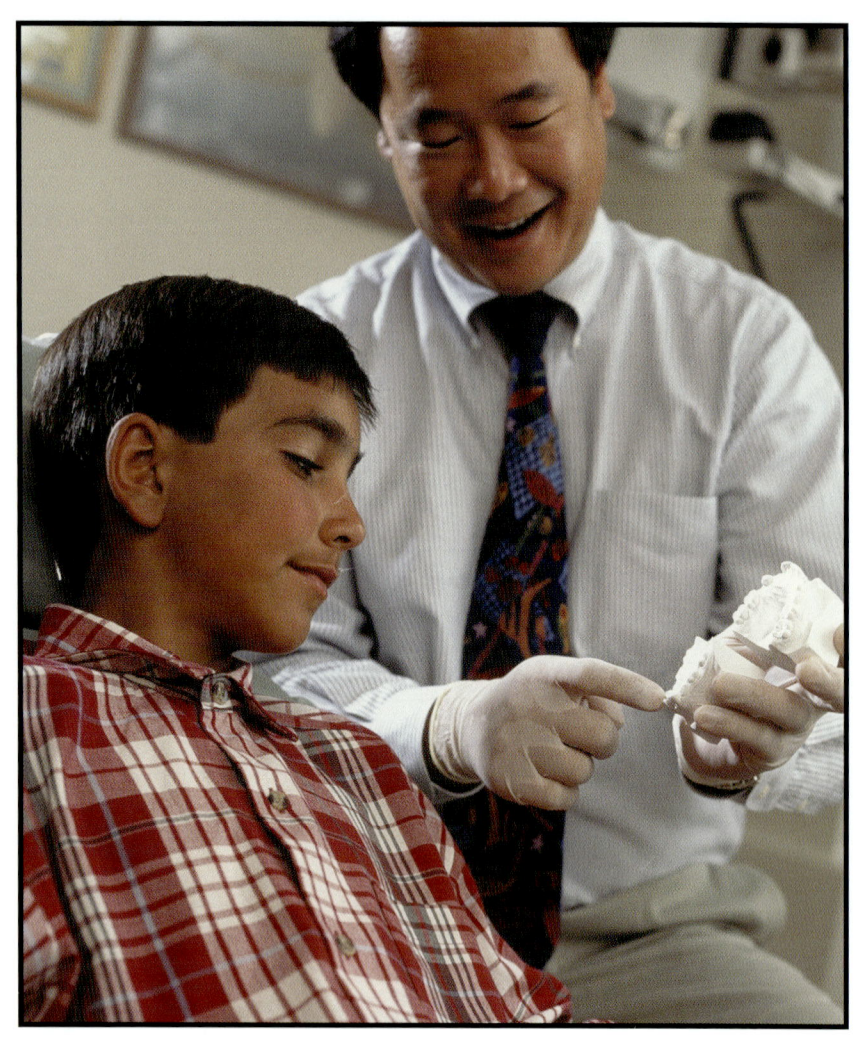

You can go to the **dentist** for **checkups**. The dentist will look at your teeth and gums to make sure they are healthy.

It's good to take care of your body. You will like the way it makes you look. You will also like the way it makes you feel—healthy!

Glossary

checkup   A meeting with a doctor to make sure you are well.

dentist   A doctor who is trained to take care of teeth and gums.

floss   To use a piece of waxy string to clean between your teeth.

germ   A tiny living thing that can make you sick.

gum   The soft, pink skin in your mouth that your teeth grow out of.

healthy   Being well.

shampoo   A special kind of soap used to wash your hair.